CESAR E. CHAVEZ

EQUAL RIGHTS LEADERS

Don McLeese

Rourke

Publishing LLC
Vero Beach, Florida 32964

PHOTO CREDITS:
All photographs from the Walter P. Reuther Library, Wayne State University

Cover Photo: *California celebrates March 31 as Cesar Chavez Day.*

EDITOR: Frank Sloan

COVER DESIGN: Nicola Stratford

Library of Congress Cataloging-in-Publication Data

McLeese, Don.
  Cesar E. Chavez / Don McLeese.
    p. cm. — (Equal rights leaders)
Includes bibliographical references and index.
Contents: The farm worker's hero—From Mexico to the United States—
Cesar's family—Cesar's schools—Moving to California—Working the
fields—United Farm Workers—Hunger strikes—Cesar lives!
  ISBN 1-58952-285-0 (hardcover)
  1. Chavez, Cesar, 1927—Juvenile literature. 2. Labor
leaders—United States—Biography—Juvenile literature. 3. United Farm
Workers—Juvenile literature. [1. Chavez, Cesar, 1927- 2. Labor leaders.
3. Mexican Americans--Biography. 4. United Farm Workers.] I. Title.

  HD6509.C48 M394 2002
  331.88'13'092--dc21   2002002042

Printed in the USA

MP/W

TABLE OF CONTENTS

The Farm Worker's Hero

Cesar E. Chavez is a hero to **Mexican-Americans** and to everyone who believes that workers should be treated fairly. He brought farm workers together into a **union**. Led by Chavez, they said they wouldn't pick grapes unless they were paid and treated better. **Grape pickers** have a better life today because of Chavez.

Cesar and farm workers

From Mexico to the United States

Cesar was named for his grandfather, Cesario Chavez. Cesario was born and lived in Mexico. He worked hard on a Mexican ranch but was very poor. In the 1880s he crossed the border into Texas, looking for a better life. He moved his whole family to Arizona, where they worked on the farms.

Cesar and his family worked the fields.

Cesar's Family

Cesar Estrada Chavez was born March 31, 1927, near Yuma, Arizona. His father was Librado Chavez, Cesario's son. His mother was named Juana. She had also moved from Mexico. Cesar was their second child and first son. Librado was a hard worker. He opened a store as well as working on the farm.

Cesar's father Librado on his 100th birthday

Cesar's Schools

The family moved around so much that Cesar once guessed that he had gone to 65 different grade schools! His family still spoke Spanish at home, as his grandfather had in Mexico. In school, they spoke only English, which made learning harder for Cesar. He quit school after the eighth grade to work in the fields.

Cesar's eighth grade graduation photo

Moving to California

The 1930s were a very bad time in the United States. This time was called the **Great Depression**, because many people were so poor. Few people had much money and many had no jobs. In 1938 the Chavez family lost its farm and moved to California. There they picked **crops** for other farms.

Cesar lived in California after the Great Depression.

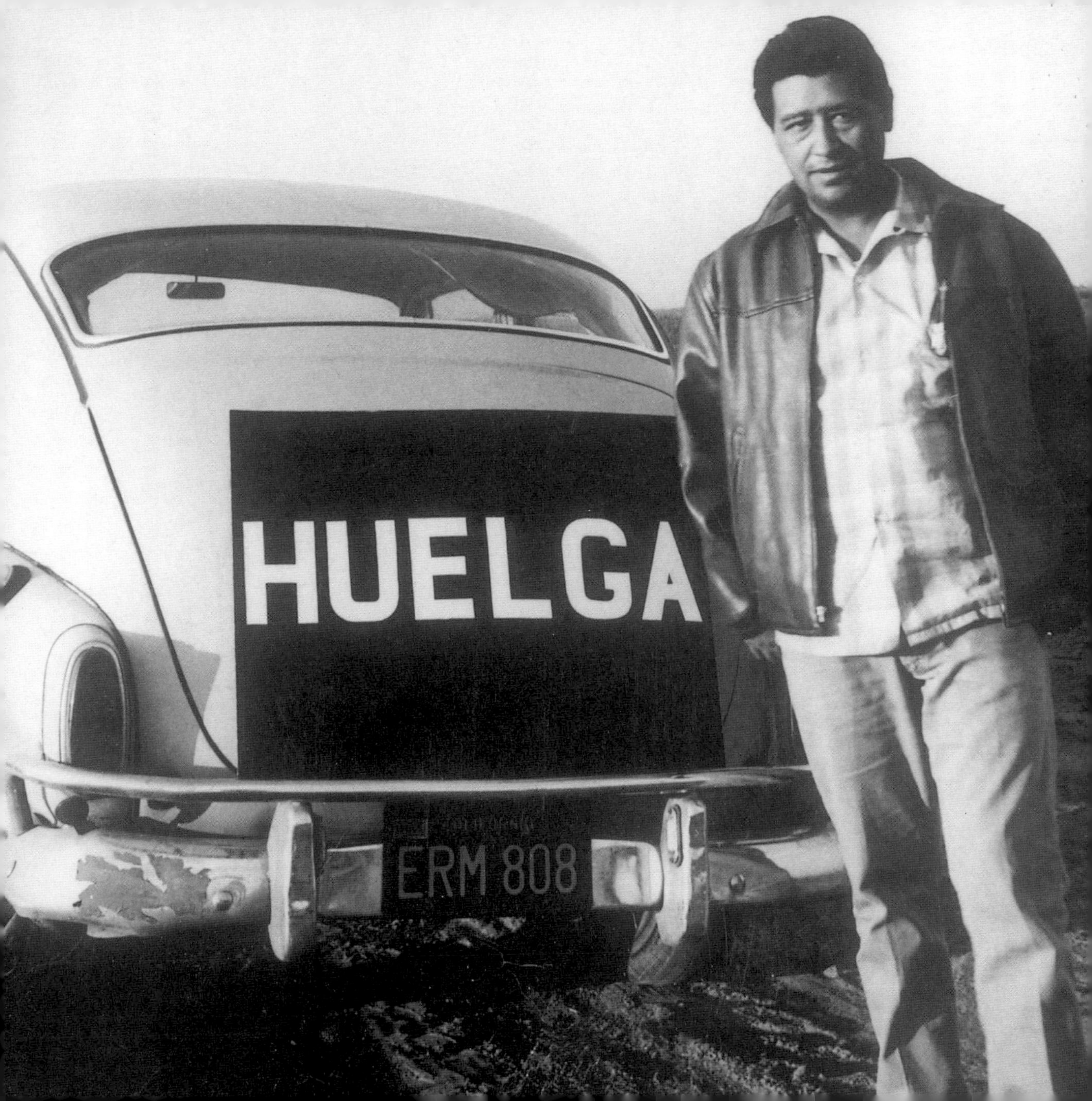
HUELGA
ERM 808

Working the Fields

During World War II, Cesar joined the Navy. When he returned from the war in 1946, he continued to pick crops in California. In 1948 he married Helen Fabela. They had eight children. It was hard to support a family with farm work, and he began to fight for change.

Cesar and Helen Chavez and six of their children

United Farm Workers

Through the 1950s and 1960s, Cesar worked with unions to make life better in the field. In 1965, he asked grape pickers to **strike**, or to refuse to work. He asked all Americans to **boycott**, or quit buying, grapes. Over the next decade, Cesar became a worker's hero as the leader of the **United Farm Workers.**

*Cesar and the United Farm
  Workers banner*

Hunger Strikes

Cesar had twice gone on **hunger strikes**, refusing to eat, and these may have weakened him. He spent his last days in Arizona, near where he was born. Throughout the Mexican-American community, he is as important as Dr. Martin Luther King, Jr., is for civil rights.

After ending his hunger strike, Cesar sat with Robert F. Kennedy.

Cesar Lives!

Cesar E. Chavez died on April 23, 1993, but his memory lives on. California celebrates March 31 as Cesar Chavez Day, making his birthday a state holiday.

In 1994, after his death, President Bill Clinton awarded him the U.S. Medal of Freedom. Every farm worker who enjoys a better life owes thanks to Cesar E. Chavez.

Cesar E. Chavez in 1991

Important Dates to Remember

1927	Cesar E. Chavez born near Yuma, Arizona, on March 31
1938	Chavez family moves to California
1946	Chavez returns from fighting in World War II
1948	Chavez marries Helen Fabela
1965	Chavez asks grape pickers to strike for better working conditions
1993	Cesar E. Chavez dies on April 23

GLOSSARY

boycott (BOY kot) — refusing to buy something or pay to use a service until workers are treated better

crops (crahps) — fruits, vegetables, or other plants that are grown on a farm and sold

grape pickers (GRAYP PICK urs) — farm workers who pick grapes

Great Depression (GRAYT de PRESH un) — the time through the 1930s when many Americans lost their jobs and had little money

hunger strikes (HUHN gur STRYKZ) — refusing to eat as a protest

Mexican-Americans (mex IH cun uh MARE ih kunz) — Americans who are from Mexico or whose relatives came from Mexico

strike (STRYK) — when a group of workers refuse to work until they get better pay and treatment

union (YEWN yun) — a group of workers who join together to get better pay and working conditions

United Farm Workers (yew NITE ed FARM WORK urz) — the farm workers union

INDEX

Further Reading

Collins, David A. *Farmworker's Friend: The Story of Cesar Chavez.* The Lerner Publishing Group, 1996.

Schaefer, Lola M. *Cesar Chavez.* Capstone Press, 1999.

Strazzabosco, Jeanne M. *Learning about Justice from the Life of Cesar Chavez.* The Rosen Publishing Group Incorporated, 1996.

Websites To Visit

http://www.sfsu.edu/~cecipp/cesar_chavez/cesarbio5-12.htm
http://latino.sscnet.ucla.edu/research/chavez/bio/

About The Author

Don McLeese is an award-winning journalist whose work has appeared in many newspapers and magazines. He is a frequent contributor to the World Book Encyclopedia. He and his wife, Maria, have two daughters and live in West Des Moines, Iowa.